THE KIDS OF EINSTEIN ELEMENTARY

THE LAST DINOSAUR

THE KIDS OF EINSTEIN ELEMENTARY
THE LAST DINOSAUR

Written by
Len Mlodinow & Matt Costello
Illustrated by **Josh Nash**

Cartwheel
·B·O·O·K·S· ®

SCHOLASTIC INC.

New York   Toronto   London   Auckland   Sydney
Mexico City   New Delhi   Hong Kong   Buenos Aires

For Nicolai
—L.M.

To my three children: Devon, Nora and
Chris, who have, in a way, travelled
through time with me.
—M.C.

Library of Congress Cataloging-in-Publication Data is available

0-439-53773-8

10 9 8 7 6 5 4 3 2 1   04 05 06 07 08
Printed in the U.S.A. 23 • First printing, July 2004

Contents

Chapter ONE

Don't call on me! Please . . . call on anyone else but . . . don't call on me! thought Kenny.

"Ken-ny," Ms. Nomer said the way she always did. "Do *you* know the answer?"

Kenny shook his head. He wasn't good at arithmetic. But that's not why he didn't want to answer. Not this time.

This time Kenny didn't want to answer because he had a giant wad of gum in his mouth.

A big class rule was "No gum." So why

did Kenny have gum in his mouth?

He forgot to get rid of it after lunch.

Ms. Nomer looked away for someone else to call on. Here was Kenny's chance. He took the gum out of his mouth. He looked at the trash can. He aimed...

But something caught Kenny's eye.

Something big and green whizzed by the door! Something with big. . . scary teeth? What was that? Was it a monster?

No, there are no monsters, Kenny told himself.

The gum missed the trash can and landed on a chair.

Kenny looked at his classmates. Had anyone else seen the big green thing? Probably not. They were all busy raising their hands to answer Ms. Nomer's question.

Just then, Mrs. Henhop, the school principal, walked through the door. A stranger stood beside her.

"This is Mr. Narly," said Mrs. Henhop. "He is from the State Office for Better Students and Teachers. He will be visiting your class today."

"Good afternoon, class," said Mr.

Narly in a squeaky voice.

"Good afternoon, Mr. Narly," the class droned.

"Mr. Narly is here to watch how you learn," Mrs. Henhop said to the class. "I'm sure he will be pleased to see your good behavior. Carry on."

She left the room.

Mr. Narly started to sit on the chair next to the trash can.

"Stop!" Kenny yelled. "You—"

"Ken-ny," said Ms. Nomer. "If you want to talk, you must raise your hand."

Kenny raised his hand. "He's about to sit on my..."

But it was too late. Mr. Narly sat right on top of the gum. He must have felt it because he tried to get back up. But Mr. Narly was stuck to the seat.

Chapter TWO

As his punishment for throwing gum on the seat, Kenny had to sit in Mrs. Henhop's office.

Kenny stared at the clock. He had watched the big hand go around once. Now it was halfway around again.

That meant he had been there for an hour and a half! It seemed like forever.

Kenny heard the final bell. At last, school was out. He got up to leave. Just then, his best friends, Steffi and José, stepped into the office.

A Picture of Time

A clock is a kind of graph because a clock is a picture of time.

1:30

Kenny started his punishment at 1:30— 30 minutes after 1:00.

1:35

When the minute hand moves from one number to the next, 5 minutes have passed.

1:30

2:00

When the minute hand moves half of the way around the clock, 30 minutes have passed. Thirty minutes are half an hour.

2:30

When the minute hand moves all the way around the clock, one hour has passed. The hour hand moves to the next number every hour.

1:30

3:00

Kenny sat for one hour and 30 minutes (an hour and a half).

"Why did you throw the gum on the seat?" asked José.

"I was aiming for the trash can," said Kenny. "But then I saw something big and scary and green running past our classroom."

"Sounds like Mrs. Grimley, the lunch lady!" said José. He laughed.

"It looked like a monster," said Kenny.

"There's no such thing as monsters," said Steffi.

Just then, they heard a strange noise outside the office. They all looked down the hall.

At the far end of the hall, they all saw a large greenish blur. It didn't look human.

Nor did it look like any other animal they had ever seen.

"Th-that sure wasn't Mrs. Grimley!" said Kenny.

"Yeah. She doesn't move fast," said José.

"She's also not green," said Steffi.

"She would be if she ever tasted her own cooking," said José. "Come on. Let's follow it!"

Chapter THREE

They followed the green shape right to the stairs that led to the school's basement.

They walked down slowly. The small, high windows let very little light into the room. Soon their eyes got used to the dark. They started to see things. They saw parts of old computers, wires, batteries, and books.

Steffi looked at a row of big blue plastic boxes with doors. They looked like the outdoor toilets they had at the park.

Kenny and José looked elsewhere.

Then José turned around. He froze!
And he said the next words very slowly.
"There's Kenny's big green monster,"
said José. He pointed.

Steffi turned her head. "No," she said. "That's not a monster. That's a struthiomimus." She sounded scared.

"A what?" said Kenny.

"It's a type of dinosaur," she whispered. "A type of carnivorous dinosaur."

"Carnivorous?" said José. "As in, 'Loves to eat people'?"

And all three of them gulped! The struthiomimus looked at them and licked its lips.

Chapter FOUR

"The struthiomimus didn't eat people," Steffi said.

"Phew!" said Kenny, feeling calmer.

"Because there weren't any people when the struthiomimus lived," Steffi said. "But I'm sure it would have eaten people . . . if it had been given the chance."

"Let's not give it a chance now," said José. And he took a small step back.

The struthiomimus saw him move. It looked at the kids—one at a time. It took a small hop. . . .

"This way!" said Steffi. "Now!"

Steffi ran to one of the big blue portable toilets. The boys followed right behind her.

"We're going to hide in a portable toilet?" said José.

"Do you have any better ideas?" said Steffi.

They squeezed into the box and shut the door fast.

A light turned on inside.

Kenny was happy to see there was no toilet, only a chair where the toilet belonged. But there was a roll of toilet paper on the wall beside it. And above that, a panel of levers and switches.

José looked at the panel. One lever had the labels HERE and THERE. Another lever had the labels NOW and THEN. And a switch had a label that read: DO NOT EVER, *EVER* THROW THIS SWITCH.

The struthiomimus charged into the side of the box. The box shook.

"How strong do you think this toilet is?" said Kenny.

"I don't think it was built for this!"

said Steffi.

The struthiomimus charged them again. Again, the box shook.

José reached for the switch.

"Don't!" said Steffi. "Can't you read the sign?"

The struthiomimus charged for the third time. Kenny fell into José. José's hand was still on the switch.

"Oops!" said José.

His hand had thrown the switch.

Chapter FIVE

The box bounced up and down. Inside the kids felt as if they were spinning, like on a carnival ride.

"Whoa! This is cool!" said José.

"Way cool!" said Kenny.

"I'm not sure being stuck in a portable toilet can be called cool," Steffi said.

Kenny glanced at the controls.

"Uh-oh," said Kenny. "I have a bad feeling about this."

"How bad?" said José.

"If this is right," said Kenny, "we're

On the time machine controls, each mark stands for 10 million years!

doing some time traveling."

"How much time traveling?" said José.

"See the small marks labeled ten, twenty, and so on?" said Kenny.

"Yeah. The lever is six and a half marks to the left," said José.

"Between the sixty and the seventy," said Kenny.

"So we went back about sixty-five years?" said José.

"No. Look what it says under the numbers," said Kenny. "The number line is counting in *millions* of years! We went back *sixty-five million* years!"

"That is silly," Steffi said. "Science says that no one can travel through time."

Two Time Lines

A number line is a kind of graph that pictures the numbers in order from left to right.

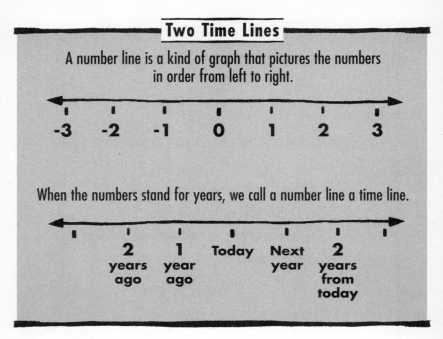

When the numbers stand for years, we call a number line a time line.

Just then, the kids heard an odd sound: ***whoosh!***

Purple smoke hid their feet. It moved in the shape of tiny tornadoes.

"What does science say about tiny purple tornadoes?" said Kenny. He tried to keep away from them.

Steffi shrugged.

How Much Is 100,000,000?

A bar graph is used to compare numbers or data.

Think of the bars in this bar graph as stacks of cards. One million (1,000,000) cards would reach as high as three of the tallest skyscrapers laid end to end. The bar for one hundred million (100,000,000) would reach to the beginnings of outer space!

| 1 | 10 | 100 |

The box was now still and quiet—both inside and out.

"I hope that the struthiomimus is gone," said Steffi.

"Or we are," said Kenny.

"There's one way to find out," said José.

He opened the door. And the struthiomimus *was* gone. The school was gone, too.

The kids slowly stepped outside. Around them were tall trees, ferns, and large flowers.

"Magnolias!" said José. "Just like the ones in our garden!"

The kids heard a whirring sound. Then they saw what made the sound— a foot-long dragonfly with purple and orange wings!

"Giant dragonflies lived in prehistoric times," Steffi said. "Just like the

struthiomimus we saw back at school. But there's no way we traveled sixty-five million years...in a portable toilet!"

Just then, a small dinosaur ran up to them. It stood only two feet tall.

"I saw a dinosaur like that in a movie," Kenny said. "A dozen more will come out and they'll eat us."

The tiny dinosaur tilted its head. It seemed to smile.

Chapter SIX

The dinosaur sat on the ground and sniffed.

"I think it's getting ready to attack!" said Kenny.

"No! I think it's crying," said Steffi. "It sounds like my cat when she's crying."

"Dinosaurs don't cry," said Kenny. "Do they?"

"No one knows for sure," said Steffi.

José walked over and petted the dinosaur.

"Its skin is really soft," he said.

"Maybe it's just a baby."

Kenny and Steffi walked over cautiously.

"Wait! It has something in its mouth," said José. He reached over to grab it.

"Don't!" said Kenny. "It will bite your fingers off!"

But the dinosaur didn't bite.

"Look!" said José.

José held a small bag of baby carrots in his hand.

"How did this get here?" he wondered.

"You see! This means we aren't back in the time of the dinosaurs," said Steffi.

Kenny sighed. "I guess we're not."

"Could we be in some kind of... dinosaur theme park?" said Steffi.

"This could be fun," said José.

The dinosaur stood up.

"I think the baby dino is lost," said

Steffi. "Let's help it find its mother."

"Better yet," said Kenny, "let's find a phone. My mom and dad won't like this at all. They don't even let me go to the corner on my own."

"We can follow the dinosaur's footprints," said Steffi. "They'll lead us back to its cage—or whatever they keep it in."

"Come on, Sammy," Steffi said to the dinosaur. "We'll get you home."

"Sammy?" asked Kenny and José.

"Yeah! I named it after my cat," said Steffi.

Kenny and José rolled their eyes.

Chapter SEVEN

The three kids and the dinosaur had to push through thick plants. They walked through sticky mud. They crossed a stream.

Meanwhile, giant dragonflies flew above them.

The kids were hot, tired, and thirsty.

"This trail is a big zigzag," José said. "It's taking forever. I just hope this zoo—or whatever it is—has snow cones!"

"I have an idea," Kenny said. "We can use the pattern of Sammy's tracks to find a shortcut."

"It's a big zigzag," said José. "That's not a pattern."

"Sure it is," said Kenny. He drew a map in the dirt. "See?"

Kenny's Map

A map is a kind of graph. A map helps us picture where we are—or where we are going. Kenny drew these maps to find the shortcut.

The Dino's Path

The Shortcut

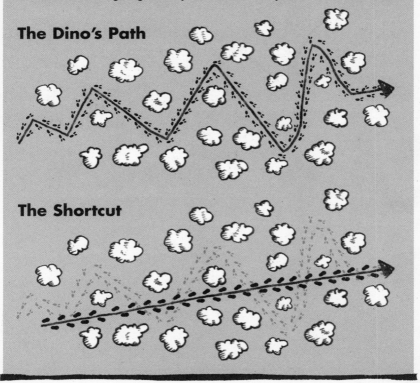

"Now I get it," said José. "Instead of following the zigzags, we can walk straight up the middle."

"Good thinking," said Steffi.

Using Kenny's new idea, the kids walked along. Soon they came to a clearing.

Now that they could see the sky, one by one, they each looked up and stared. Even Sammy. What they saw was a giant, red ball of fire. It looked much bigger and brighter than the sun.

And the fireball was falling—falling right toward them!

Chapter
EIGHT

"It's the asteroid!" Steffi said.

"What's an asteroid?" said José.

"An asteroid is like a giant rock that travels around the sun," Steffi said. "About sixty-five million years ago— I mean sixty-five million years before the time we came from—an asteroid hit Earth."

"And that is about the time we're in now," Kenny said.

"You win," said Steffi. "No theme park could ever fake this."

"What happened after the asteroid hit Earth?" Kenny asked.

"First there was a big crash," Steffi said. "Then came huge fires and tidal waves. Then there was acid rain. Dust darkened the earth for many years, so the plants died. Then the animals that ate those plants died, too."

"It's like the food chain Ms. Nomer told us about," said José.

"More like the end of the food chain," said Kenny.

"Exactly," said Steffi. "But somehow, smaller animals had an easier time, and they survived."

"They ate the leftovers," José said with a small laugh.

No one else laughed, though.

"Do you mean that small animals

like us didn't die?" Kenny asked
hopefully.

"No," said Steffi. "Smaller than us."

"So what you're saying is—we're
doomed," said Kenny.

Chapter NINE

Kenny looked at his watch. It was 2:00. He put up his fingers and used them to measure the asteroid's size. It was one finger wide. He didn't know what that meant in real size. Maybe miles. Maybe the asteroid was as big as their town!

The little dinosaur started to run away. Did it sense the danger?

Steffi ran after it.

"Stop!" yelled Kenny. "We have to get back home!"

But Steffi kept running.

"We have to get Steffi," José said.

Kenny nodded. He put his fingers up toward the sky again. Now the asteroid was *more* than one finger wide. It was coming closer fast!

Chapter

TEN

Steffi ran after the dinosaur. And José and Kenny ran after Steffi.

They ran past giant flowers, plants, and insects.

They ran past an alamosaurus—taller than their school and almost half as long.

They ran past a styracosaurus with horns as big as a person.

They ran until they reached sand. Beyond them they saw the ocean.

The kids were almost too tired to run. Luckily, the dinosaur was tired, too.

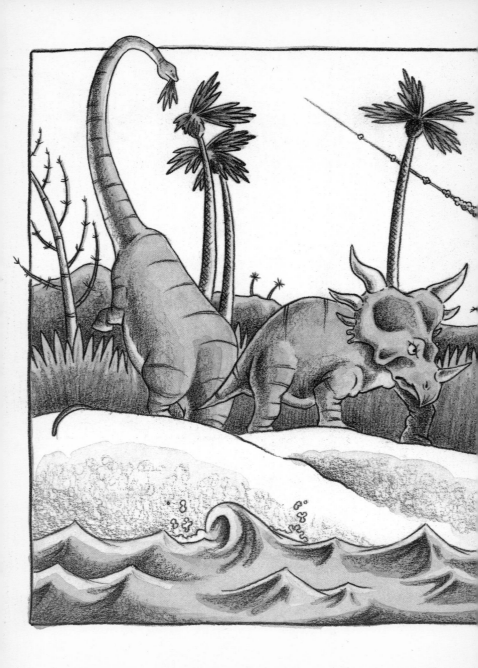

It fell on the sand.

The kids fell down next to it.

"Bad dinosaur!" Steffi said. "Where do you think you're going?" Then she gave the dinosaur a big hug.

José pointed to the sky. "Look!" he said. The others looked up.

A large animal was flying over the ocean. It looked like a pelican. But it was the size of an airplane.

"A pteranodon!" Steffi said.

But Kenny looked beyond the huge pteranodon. He put up his fingers again.

Then he checked his watch. It was 2:32.

He said, "Guys, the asteroid is as big as two fingers now. It's doubled in size. We've got to get out of here now!"

"Let's go, Sammy," said José. "You're coming with us!"

Chapter ELEVEN

With Kenny leading the way, the kids and the dinosaur hurried back to the time machine. Now and then, Kenny looked up and measured the asteroid. It went from two fingers to three, then to three and a half fingers wide.

Finally, the kids saw the big blue toilet time machine.

Next to it stood another time machine.

And next to that stood the struthiomimus that had chased them here!

"What do we do now?" José asked.

Kenny measured the asteroid. It was four fingers wide.

"We wait for the struthiomimus to go away," Steffi said. "We don't want to be its dinner."

So they waited. The asteroid turned five fingers wide. Then...six fingers wide.

"We've got to get into the time machine now," Kenny said. "We can't wait anymore."

"I bet we can wait ten or twenty minutes more," said José.

"No, we can't," said Kenny.

He drew a table in the dirt. "When I first measured the asteroid, it was one finger wide. After thirty-two minutes, it was two fingers wide. Sixteen minutes later, it was four fingers wide. Eight minutes after that, it was eight fingers wide."

Kenny's Table

Kenny made a table of the asteroid's size. He found a pattern.
Can you see it?

Time since last look (in minutes)	Start	32	16	8	4	2
Size of asteroid (in fingers)	1	2	4	8	16	?

Kenny looked up. An hour had now
passed since they first saw the asteroid. It
had taken Kenny four minutes to explain
his table and graph. The asteroid was now
so big that Steffi had to help him measure
it. It was sixteen fingers across!

"The pattern shows that in two more
minutes, it will be thirty-two fingers across,"
Kenny said. "It will be right on top of us.
Struthiomimus or no struthiomimus—

49

we've got to go right now!"

The kids and the little dinosaur raced toward the time machine.

When they got close to the struthiomimus, they saw it looked sick. The reason was spilling out of a big pot in the second time machine. It was chili from the school cafeteria!

"That would make anything sick," said José.

"Whoever brought the struthiomimus back must have been feeding it chili," said Steffi.

"Yeah, so it won't attack," said Kenny.

"It won't attack, but it might throw up," said José.

"Let's go!" said Steffi.

By now, the asteroid filled the sky. Trees were burning.

The kids stuffed themselves and the

little dinosaur into the time machine. Kenny set the levers to HERE and NOW.

"No!" said Steffi.

"No?" asked Kenny and José.

"First we're going back one hundred years. Sammy will be safe and happy there."

Kenny set the lever back.

The children left Sammy in a safe place—one hundred years before the asteroid. Then they hugged him good-bye and raced back into the time machine.

Finally, they hoped, they were on their way home.

"I have just one question," José said to Steffi. "How did the magnolias survive the asteroid?"

Steffi thought about it. "Seeds don't need light. So the seeds could survive. Then when the light came back, the seeds could sprout and grow."

"Seeds are awesome," said José. And
he threw the switch.

Chapter TWELVE

José opened the door. Once again, they saw the basement full of tools, books, computer parts, and outdoor toilets.

"Whose stuff is this?" Steffi said.

"I don't know. But I bet it's the same person who left the bag of carrots back in prehistoric times," Kenny said.

"I'd like to find him—or her— sometime," said Steffi. "I have a lot of questions!"

"Well, I'm ready to go home," said José. "Let's get out of here."

"Not so fast," said Kenny. He looked at his watch. "It's still only 3:05. We came back the same time we started."

"Time for after-school activities," said Steffi.

"You can help me with my math," said Kenny.

"Hey, hold on!" said Steffi. "You still think you're 'bad' at math?"

Kenny nodded.

"Who figured out a way to get through the jungle faster?" said José.

"That wasn't really math," said Kenny.

"Patterns are math," said Steffi.

"And who figured out we had only two minutes left, when I thought we had twenty?" said José.

"You used data for that. And graphing," said Steffi. "That's math for sure! In fact, it is what you'll need to know for *algebra*."

"Wow!" said Kenny. "I guess I am good at some parts of math! Just not arithmetic."

"Well, I'm good at that," said Steffi.

"What a team!" said José.

"A team that will someday figure out what this is all about, okay?" said Steffi.

"Okay," said Kenny.

"I promise," said José.

"But for now—time for me to finish my homework," said Kenny.

"Time for my snow cone," said José.

The kids raced out of the dark, musty basement and into the bright hallway of Einstein Elementary. Steffi looked out the window at a magnolia tree in bloom. They and the magnolia had something in common, she thought. They had all survived the asteroid. And thanks to her and her friends, so had a dinosaur named Sammy.

About the Authors

Leonard Mlodinow is the author of the critically acclaimed books for adults, *Feynman's Rainbow: A Search for Beauty in Physics and in Life* and *Euclid's Window: The Story of Geometry from Parallel Lines to Hyperspace.* He has also written episodes of television shows, including *Star Trek: The Next Generation* and *MacGyver,* and created award-winning game software for Disney and Scholastic. Mr. Mlodinow holds a PhD in mathematical physics from UC Berkeley.

Matt Costello's bestselling and award-winning work meshes game play, technology, and story. His credits include multimedia projects such as *Aladdin's Mathquest* for Disney Interactive; *Clifford's Adventure* for Scholastic; and *Barbie's Riding Club.* He is also a cocreator of ZoogDisney. An author of adult books, his latest novel is *Missing Monday* from Penguin Putnam. In addition, Mr. Costello is a teacher of gifted and talented students in New York State.

Another exciting story about
The Kids from Einstein Elementary!

Steffi, Kenny, and José want to visit Sammy at the time of the dinosaurs. They sneak into one of the time machines. José throws the switch. And once again they are traveling though time and space.

But something is wrong. The controls aren't set for prehistoric times. Where are they going?

When the machine stops, Jose is the first to step outside. They seem to be in an old-fashioned bedroom. But this is not an ordinary room. This is a room on a ship. And that ship is the *Titanic* and it is going to sink!

On the ship, the kids make friends with a girl named Emma and her cat.

The kids also make some enemies!

Read more about The Kids from Einstein Elementary in…

Titanic Cat!

You'll find it wherever books are sold!